Pickles Helps Out

by Michèle Dufresne

PIONEER VALLEY EDUCATIONAL PRESS, INC.

Danny and Amy
were making a cake.
Pickles wanted to help.
"Woof, woof," said Pickles.

"Go away, Pickles.
We are busy," said Amy.
"We can't play now."

Mom was folding the laundry.
Pickles wanted to help.
"Woof, woof," said Pickles.

Pickles climbed into the basket.
"Oh, no!" said Mom. "Go away!
You are getting my laundry dirty."

Dad was washing the car.
Pickles wanted to help.
"Woof, woof," said Pickles.

"Pickles, you will get all wet.
Go away," said Dad.

Pickles was sad.
She wanted to help.

A little boy was walking
down the street. He was crying.
"I'm lost," the boy said
to Pickles.

Pickles ran to Dad.
"Woof, woof!"
"Woof, woof, woof!"

"What's the matter, Pickles?"
asked Dad.
Pickles ran back
to the little boy.
Dad followed her.

"I am lost!" said the boy.
"I can't find my mom!"

Dad looked at Pickles.
"Pickles, can you help me find
this little boy's mom?"

"Woof, woof, woof," said Pickles.